DATE DUE

WILSON GAGE

Squash Pie

pictures by GLEN ROUNDS

GREENWILLOW BOOKS

A Division of William Morrow & Company, Inc.
New York

Library of Congress Cataloging in Publication Data
Squash pie. (Read-alone series)
Summary: Time after time the farmer plants squash for
his favorite pie, only to have someone steal every crop.
I. Rounds, Glen (date)   II.   Title.   PZ7.S8146Sq [E]
75-29157   ISBN 0-688-80031-9   ISBN 0-688-84031-0 lib. bdg.

To William
in gratitude for the
seeing-eye potato
and  with love

Once there was a farmer
who wanted to grow squash.
He wanted to grow squash
because he liked squash pie.
He liked squash pie better than
apple pie or cherry pie
or any other kind of pie.

In the spring

he plowed his garden.

He planted tomatoes, beans and peas.

He planted beets, pumpkins and squash.

The sun shone and the rain fell.

The vegetables began to grow.

The tomatoes began to turn red.

Soon the squash were ready to pick.

"Tomorrow I will pick the squash,"

the farmer said to his wife.

"Then we will have squash pie."

But the next morning
the squash were gone.
During the night
someone had stolen every one.

The farmer was mad.

He was furious.

He threw his hat on the ground
and jumped on it.

"Someone has stolen
all my squash!" he yelled.

"How can I have squash pie
without a squash?"

"Never mind," said his wife.

"I will make an apple pie."

"And I will plant more squash,"
said the farmer.

The farmer's wife baked.

The farmer planted squash.

He also planted potatoes

all over the place.

"Why are you planting
so many potatoes?"
asked his wife.
"Potatoes have eyes,"
answered the farmer.
"They will watch carefully.
When my squash are big
and ready to be picked,
the potatoes will keep
a good lookout.
They will see the thief coming.
I will be able to stop him
before he steals my squash."

The sun shone and the rain fell.

The carrots grew long and orange.

The squash began to get big.

"Tomorrow we will pick the squash,"
the farmer told his wife.
"Then we will have squash pie."

But the next morning
when the farmer went
to pick his squash,
they were all gone.
During the night
someone had stolen every one.

The farmer was so mad he yelled!

He picked up a big stick

and hit the ground with it.

He hit the ground very hard.

"Someone has stolen
all the squash!"
he screamed.
"How can I have squash pie
without any squash?"

The farmer's wife came running

to see what was the matter.

"Didn't the potatoes see the thief?"
she asked.

"No," the farmer answered.

"The thief came when it was dark.
Besides, the potatoes' eyes
were under the ground."

"Never mind," said his wife.

"I will make a cherry pie."

"And I will plant more squash,"
said the farmer.
The farmer planted squash.
He also planted rows and rows
of corn.

"Why are you planting
so many rows of corn?"
asked his wife.

CORN

"Corn has ears,"

the farmer answered.

"When the thief comes

to steal my squash,

the corn will be listening.

It will hear him

open the garden gate.

"Then I will be able to catch him
before he steals a single squash.
The ears will hear the thief
even if he comes at night
when the potatoes cannot see."

The days went by.

Soon the squash were ready to pick.

"Squash pie!" cried the farmer.

"Tomorrow I will pick my squash.

Tomorrow I will have squash pie."

But the next morning

the farmer's wife heard such a noise.

She ran to the garden.

The farmer was jumping up and down.

He was yelling and screaming.

He was hitting the ground

with a big stick.

"What has happened?"

cried the farmer's wife.

"My squash!" yelled the farmer.

"All my squash are gone.

There is not one squash

left for squash pie!"

During the night

someone had stolen every one.

"Didn't the ears of corn

hear the thief open the gate?"

asked the farmer's wife.

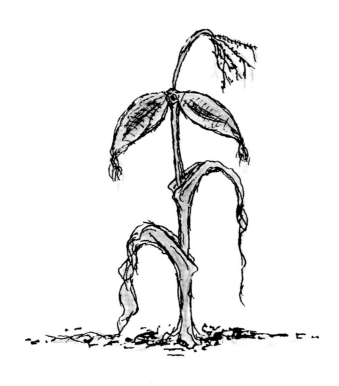

"Yes," the farmer answered.
"They heard the gate squeak.
But corn cannot talk.
The corn could not tell us
that the thief was coming."

"That is too bad,"

said the farmer's wife.

"I will bake a berry pie."

"I do not want a berry pie,"

said the farmer.

"I want a squash pie.

I will plant more squash."

And he did.

The corn's ears
had not heard him.
The dogwood's bark
had not scared him.

"No squash," sobbed the farmer.

"There, there," said his wife.

"You shall have squash pie."

She picked up some big ripe peaches
and threw them high in the air.
They came down—SQUASH!

She took them into the kitchen
and made a squash pie.

"Oh, this is good," said the farmer.

"It certainly is," said the farmer's wife.

"I have been wrong all this time.

I thought squash pie

would taste awful.

This pie tastes wonderful!"

So the farmer and his wife together
planted lots of squash.

It grew very fast.

No one stole a single squash.

When the squash were ripe,

the farmer and his wife picked them.

Together they made nine pies.

The farmer's wife
tasted the biggest pie.
"Goodness," she said.
"This pie is even better
than that other squash pie I made.
That other squash pie
tasted just like a peach pie.
This squash pie
tastes better than peach pie.
It tastes better than
apple pie or cherry pie or
any other kind of pie.
Let's eat them all."

And they did.

DATE DUE

12-76

1986

jE